# Topspin

by

Sean Callery

Illustrated by Aleksandar Sotirovski

I learned to hit topspin and play better tennis from a great coach called Steve Bone. Thank you, Steve!

With special thanks to:

Josh Allinson
Anne Bergin
Rebecca Brant
Frances Burrage
Jake Cam
Yasmin Ewers
Nick Goldsborough
George Howlett
Harry Leighfield
Billy Mullins
Rachel Nalletamby
Sam Nalletamby
Louise Narrios
Sarah Norris
Kirstie Tracey
Shane Walker
Bradley Yendall
Max Yendall
Tom Wiltshire



First published in 2010 in Great Britain by
Barrington Stoke Ltd
18 Walker St, Edinburgh, EH3 7LP

www.barringtonstoke.co.uk



ISBN: 978-1-84299-827-4

Printed in Great Britain by Bell & Bain Ltd

# Contents

# Chapter 1
# Place, Not Pace

"Not again!" Tim hit the tennis ball far too hard and it sailed over the fence. It just missed a woman who was walking past the sports centre office. He bashed his racket against his leg.

"You're trying too hard," said his dad. "Relax. Try to brush the strings of your racquet across the ball and turn your wrist. That's how you get topspin on the ball ..."

"Yeah. I know."

The woman smiled, picked up the ball and threw it over the fence at Dad. He hit it away with his racket and grinned at her as she walked on. *Dad doesn't smile much these days*, thought Tim

"OK, lads, that's all the serving done," said Dad to the six boys he was coaching. "What do we say about where to hit the ball?"

"It's not the pace, it's the place!" Tim called out with the other players. His dad set up the next drill and they started to hit balls at the red cones placed in the corners of the court. The other boys – even Nat, who didn't like him – cheered when Tim knocked one over.

"Get the ball behind the other player to make it hard for him," called his dad. "OK, that's it for today, lads, see you next week."

As they got in the car Dad said, “Don’t worry about that topspin serve. We’ve made a start on it. And your topspin drive is much better now.” He looked into the window of the sports centre as they drove away from the tennis courts. The woman waved.

As they drove home Tim turned his wrist as you should to hit a topspin drive. It puts spin on the ball and makes it loop high over the net as if it is going miles out. Then the ball drops fast and bounces long and high. He knew how hard it was to hit shots like that back.

If he could hit it well more often, Dad might think he was OK to enter the tennis tournament next month.

Then his world fell apart.

"Listen, son, I've got something to tell you." Dad's eyes stayed on the road. "I'm leaving your mother."

Tim said nothing.

"You must have seen we aren't happy.
I've met someone else. I'm moving out."

# Chapter 2
# Going, Going, Gone

Tim watched his dad load the last few boxes into his car.

He really was leaving.

"You haven't got all your gear," said Mum.

*Maybe he isn't going for long?* thought Tim.

"Don't worry, Kate. I'll pick up some more of my stuff when I drop Tim off from tennis," said Dad.

Tim shouted at his dad to hide his tears. "Forget it. I'm not playing tennis any more!"

"But you're good," his dad said. "We just need to keep – "

"Keep what? Trying?" shouted Mum. "You're not trying to stay with me, are you?"

Dad left.

Tim's sister Holly waved sadly as Dad's car engine revved. Then she went upstairs and clicked on her computer.

Mum went to her room and slammed the door.

Tim switched on the TV.

Only Holly went along when Dad came to take them out later in the week. Tim was too angry with his dad even to open the door to him.

That evening Holly knocked on Tim's bedroom door saying, "There's a letter for you."

It was the entry form for the tennis tournament. Dad must have put his name down for it.

"I won't play," he muttered.

"Didn't think you would," said Holly.

"How did you know what it was?"

"Dad told me," she said.

"How can you even talk to him after what he's done?" asked Tim.

"He's still my dad. I want him to be happy, and he wasn't," said Holly. "He's picking me up again tomorrow."

Tim slammed his bedroom door shut.

"He said you could come if you like," she called.

When Dad knocked at the door the next day, Tim didn't come out.

# Chapter 3
# Fish Fingers or Pizza?

Tim was looking in the freezer for a pack of fish fingers when Holly came home. She pushed the freezer door shut.

"It's always fish fingers or pizza," she moaned.

"It's what Mum said to cook," said Tim.

"Yes, but she's not thinking right at the moment, is she?" said Holly. "You're fifteen and I'm twelve. We can manage better than this. I'm going to find out how to cook something else. I'll have a look on the internet."

Tim didn't like it, but she was right.

Ten minutes later Holly came out of her room holding a print-out from a cookery site, and they went to the shops together. The rice they made was soggy and the chicken burned, but it was still better than more fish fingers or pizza. Mum had some food in her room.

“Yummy,” said Holly. “We’ll try pasta tomorrow.”

That was what Dad liked to cook.

Tim and Holly looked at each other.

"I miss him doing funny voices, and I miss showing him what I can do on the computer," Holly said. "Dad makes you feel so good."

Tim thought about the coaching lessons where everyone tried hard to get a "Well done" from his dad.

"He's happier now he's with Sally," said Holly.

"Who's Sally?" Tim asked.

"She works at the sports centre."

She must be the woman who threw his ball back over the fence. Maybe that was why Dad had been so keen to get him playing tennis. He wanted to see more of her. Tim said a rude word.

"But he's sad you're not playing tennis."

Tim said the rude word again.

# Chapter 4
# No Match

Tim sat on his bed and hit a few pretend shots with his tennis racket.

Punch. Punch. That's how Dad said to hit them.

He'd like to punch Dad.

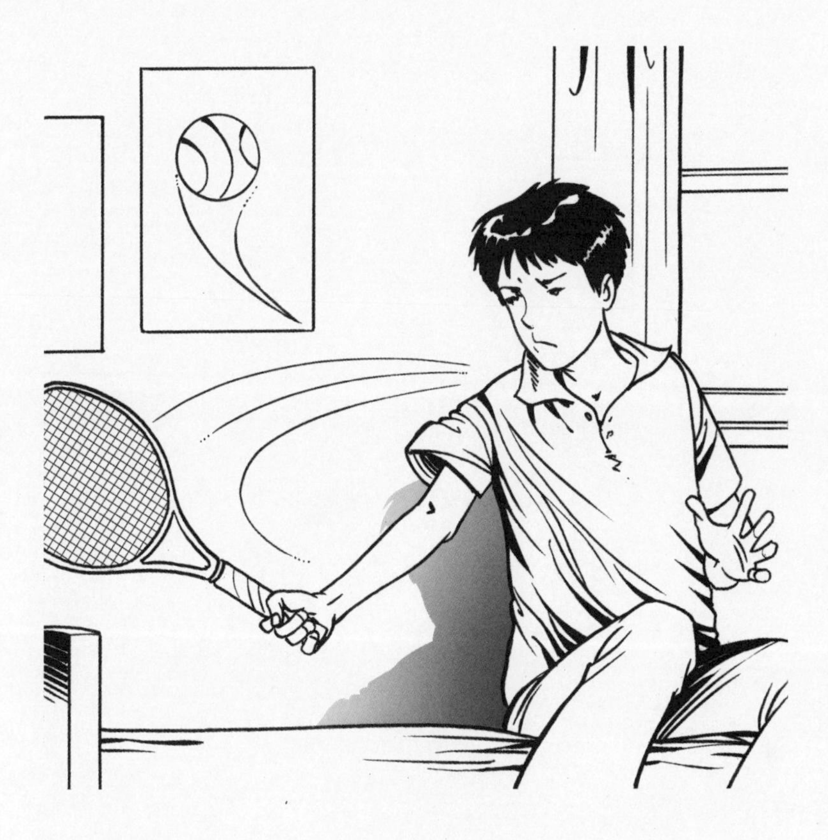

But he had missed playing all week. He loved the feel of the ball flying off the strings. Holly said that Dad was going away with Sally for the weekend. So he wouldn't be at the courts. Maybe he'd go and hit a few serves ...

He'd hit most of the spare balls when Nat turned up and started whacking them back.

"Want a game?" called Nat. He was jogging on the spot to warm up.

They were about as good as each other. Nat hit the ball hard and deep, but Tim knew how to bend his knees to keep firm on his feet and crack the ball back.

When Tim got a first serve in, Nat had problems with its speed. But if Tim missed it and had to do a second serve, Nat hit it hard for a winner. In tennis you often win if you are first to get to the net because it's easier to hit a winning shot from there. Nat did just that, rushing up to the net behind his shots nearly every time. When they shook hands, only Nat was smiling. Tim hated losing.

"Well played," he said.

"Yeah, you too." Tim had already turned towards the gate.

He was surprised when Holly opened it.

"You could beat him," she said.

"Oh, yeah?" he snapped. What did she know? She'd never even been to watch him play before.

"He gets to the net, and he's tall," she said. "So don't lob it over his head. You should hit it low and to the side."

“How did you get to be such an expert?” snapped Tim.

“I’ve been looking on the web,” she said. “It’s very interesting.”

Tim picked up his bag and walked off so fast she had to run to keep up.

He didn't like losing.

He didn't like being told what to do by his sister.

And he didn't like her being right.

# Chapter 5
# The Coaching Team

Tim went to ask his mum if she was coming out of her room today.

"I just need a bit more time," she said in a shaky voice. "I'm sorry. I know it's not fair you doing all the work."

Her eyes were wet.

“It’s OK, Mum,” he said softly. “I don’t mind.”

She asked him to check Holly had done her homework.

When he went to his sister’s room, she wasn’t at the computer for once. She was kneeling on the floor bending the right arm of a plastic doll round its head.

"I thought you didn't play with Blondie any more," he said.

"I don't. I'm working out how to hit a topspin serve," said his sister.

"You're doing what?" said Tim.

"You need it for your, what-do-you-call-it, back-up service."

"For my second serve. How do you know what to do?"

Holly tapped the keyboard and the screen lit up with an image of a tennis player.

She showed him on her computer how the server threw the ball high over his left shoulder. Then he bent his back and hit the ball.

"That's what I'm doing with Blondie."

Tim watched the screen as the ball looped high in the air and kicked up when it bounced.

“It would be cool if you did that,” said Holly.

She made him fill in the tennis form, got a stamp off Mum and went out to post it herself. So Tim now had a coaching team: a pint-sized 12-year-old girl and a plastic doll called Blondie.

# Chapter 6
# A Bucket of Balls

When Tim came down for breakfast, Holly was already onto her second bowl of cornflakes. He noticed that her fingers looked purple.

"You should be careful with those felt tips," he said.

"Good morning, Grumpy-face. Shall we practise that serve today?" she asked.

Tim frowned. He needed to work on his serve. But he didn't want to do it at the tennis courts in case he met his dad. He also didn't want Nat to know what he was doing. He didn't know any posh people with their own courts who he could ask.

Holly had the answer.

"We'll need to do it in the back garden where no one can see. I've got it ready."

Tim looked out and saw a line of purple chalk at the same level as a tennis net along the garage wall.

He was about to point out that they didn't have any tennis balls to practise with, but Holly read his mind.

"There's a bucket of balls outside the back door."

He looked. There they were. This stuff costs money. Where had she got it from? Had she stolen it from the sports centre?

"Let's just say that Blondie found them," was all she would say.

Soon there were balls all over the garden, not counting the ones that had gone over the fence. One even sailed over the roof of the house. Tim was still finding the serve really hard.

Each time he hit a ball, Holly watched. She always had a comment:

"Throw the ball up to your left."

"Hit across the ball."

"You need to hit up."

"Push from your back leg."

It felt really odd to hit the ball that way but he was getting the hang of it.

They shared a drink, and then Holly said, "OK. I'll send you balls for the topspin drive."

“You sound like a real tennis coach,” he said.

Holly smiled. “It was on the same website. It looks easier than the serve.”

She threw a ball and he bent his knees and swept his racket back and round, turning his wrist to put spin on the ball. It looped up and fell fast to hit the garage wall.

They practised out in the garden every other day for two weeks. Sometimes they saw Mum watching them from her window. She looked half asleep. When Tim slept he could hear his sister saying, “Hit up and across the ball” in his dreams.

The more he practised, the less often a ball flew wildly off. But he still made mistakes. One bad shot hit Holly in the face and she had to try really hard not to cry.

They finished early that day.

Was he good enough to beat Nat tomorrow?

# Chapter 7
# The Tournament

It was the day of the tournament. Tim's tummy felt like a bouncing ball. Holly looked up at him as they hurried to the courts.

"Of course you're jumpy. But you'll be fine."

When they arrived she went to check who he was going to play first. Tim ran on the spot to warm up. She put her phone away as she came back.

"You've got Ravi. You need to hit the ball at his feet."

How did she know that? Was she right? Tim tried it out during the warm up on court and it worked. When he had a wide shot, Ravi struck it back well. But when Tim hit his topspin drive to dip the ball at his feet, Ravi messed up every time.

The match was easy. Tim made it through the next two rounds to reach the final against Nat. It was the best of three sets.

"Keep thinking. Go for angles. Don't be put off by anyone," said Holly, putting her phone away.

Who had she been talking to? Then Tim saw his dad walk round the courts and sit on a bench behind him. Dad gave him the thumbs up. He knew then why Holly had been on the phone so much.

Tim turned away.

Now every shot he hit either fell into the net or blasted the back fence. Nat easily took the first set.

Tim munched on a banana and tried to forget dad was there. Then he thought, *What would Dad say?*

*It's the place, not the pace.*

Tim started flicking the ball to the sides of the court. Nat panted as he reached for the wide shots. Tim kept doing it and took the second set.

He was so aware that they were in the final set that he went to pieces. He could hardly lift his racket. His mind had gone blank. Two serves went way out. Double fault. Then another miss. When Tim hit a weak second serve, Nat blasted the short ball for a winner.

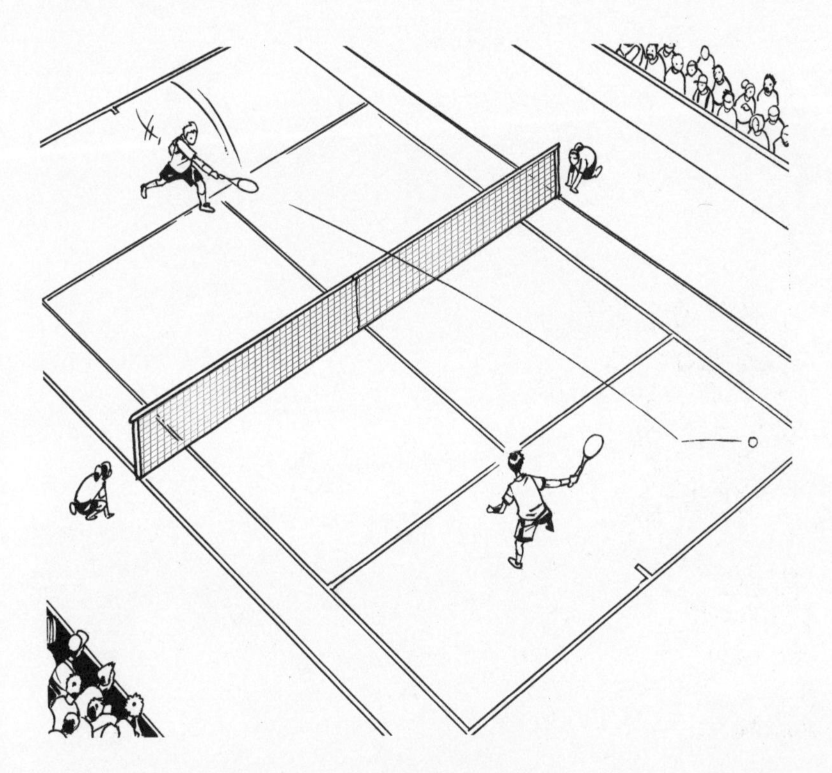

Then it came back to Tim. "Hit up and across the ball," he said as he threw the ball wide over his left shoulder and struck it side-ways with his racket. Nat watched, amazed, as it landed just in front of him and kicked up past his shoulder.

"Again!" shouted Holly.

*She's right*, Tim thought. *Keep hitting that topspin serve*.

Nat's body began to give way as he tired. He lost confidence and started to make mistakes.

Tim was thinking so hard about each point that he lost track of the score. He hit a topspin drive back behind Nat and was walking back to the line to serve again when loud clapping made him jump.

“You’ve done it, Tim!” Holly was jumping up and down. “That was match point!”

Dad was next to her, smiling, and there was Mum behind him, clapping.

“Great play, son. That topspin serve worked a treat,” said Dad.

“It’s all thanks to Holly,” said Tim.

“No, it’s thanks to Dad,” said Holly. “You didn’t really think I could have come up with all those tips on my own? I had a bit of help.” She smiled up at her father.

"You've been helping him?" said his mother.

"Just some balls to practise with and a few text messages," said Dad. "Anyway, I'll leave you to it."

As he turned to go, Tim called out, "Dad ... thanks. Are you still coaching at the weekend?"

"I'm up at the courts every Saturday, Tim. It would be great if you came." Dad turned to Mum. "Look, Kate, I could have done things better. Can we talk?"

There was a pause. Then Mum smiled and nodded.

"I think it's time I got going again," she said. "What do you fancy for tea tonight, kids?"

"Not fish fingers or pizza," said Tim and Holly together.

# *Extreme Race*

## by

## Jane A. C. West

Mark and Ben plan to run 150 miles, across the Sahara desert, to raise money for Ben's sick sister. Will they survive sandstorms, sunburn, freezing nights and 40°C days – and finish the race?

# *The Dancing Stones*

**by**

**Maggie Pearson**

They say if you dance round the stones at midnight you'll be turned to stone. Kelly thinks it's rubbish, and she's going to prove it. But Ben's worried. What if she's wrong?

You can order *The Dancing Stones* from our website at www.barringtonstoke.co.uk

# *The Dunkirk Escape*

## by

## Jim Eldridge

Dave Jones is trapped on the beach at Dunkirk, as bombs explode all around him. Can his son Tom get there in time to save him?

**by**

**S. P. Gates**

Levi is in danger. There's a killer croc on the loose – and it's hungry! Can he escape its jaws?

You can order *Killer Croc* from our website at www.barringtonstoke.co.uk